The Krow Twins
in The Da Finchi Code

by J.D. Smith

The Krows

in The Da Finchi Code

MOGZILLA

First published by Mogzilla in 2011
Paperback edition
ISBN: 978-1-906132-026

Text copyright J.D. Smith
Cover by Rachel de Ste. Croix
Cover ©Mogzilla 2010
Illustrations by Craig Conlan
Printed in the UK

Author's acknowledgements:
The journey from imagination to page is not an easy one, and many people have helped The Krow Twins along. My special thanks go to Brian Asbury (an undisputed 'bird' expert) for his editing, comments and guidance and Debbie Hepplewhite for her constant support and encouragement.

http://www.mogzilla.co.uk/krows

For my Mum – an inspirational woman

MEET THE BIRDS:

THE KROWS

THE CRIME RATE IN WYRE WOOD IS HIGHER THAN A STORK'S ARMPIT, AND THE KROW TWINS ARE BEHIND MOST OF IT!

- TOMMY KROW – TWIN BROTHER TO TERRY, HE'S THE LEADER OF THE GANG.

- TERRY KROW – ALTHOUGH HE HATCHED A FEW MINUTES BEFORE TOMMY, HE ALWAYS DOES WHATEVER HIS BROTHER SAYS.

- MOTHER KROW – THE REAL POWER IN THE KROWS' NEST. TOMMY AND TERRY WORSHIP THEIR DEAR OLD MA AND WOULD DO ANYTHING FOR HER. ESPECIALLY IF IT'S SOMETHING DODGY. KNOW WHAT I MEAN?

- LEONARDO DA FINCHI – A KEY MEMBER OF THE KROWS' GANG. HE'S A MASTER FORGER, COPIER AND ART THIEF. IN FACT A TRUE ARTIST IN CRIME.

- DWAYNE THE 'CHAVVINCH' ALTHOUGH HE WORKS FOR THE KROWS, THIS SPECTACULARLY SILLY CHAFFINCH IS TERRIFIED OF TOMMY AND TERRY.

- BRIAN AND DEREK – TWO BULLYING BUZZARDS WITH JUST ONE BIRD BRAIN BETWEEN THEM. CAN YOU GUESS WHICH ONE IS USING IT NOW?

BIRD POLICE FORCE

- DETECTIVE BIRD INSPECTOR (DBI) GEORGE HOOT – A GRUMPY, OLD-FASHIONED TAWNY OWL. HOOT HAS MADE IT TO THE TOP OF THE TREE AND IS NOW IN CHARGE OF WYRE WOOD POLICE STATION.

- Bird Constable (BC) Florisa Starling – Fresh out of Police Training School, this is her first job. Florisa is so keen to impress everyone, she's even decorated her uniform with glitter.

- Bird Constable (BC) Jane Sparrow – an elderly tree sparrow who keeps the police station running like clockwork. Fond of peanuts, Jane always loves a good gossip.

- The Sparrowhawk Patrol – this brave team of fast flyers are often first to the scene of a crime. They work for DBI Hoot of course.

VICTIM OF THE CRIME

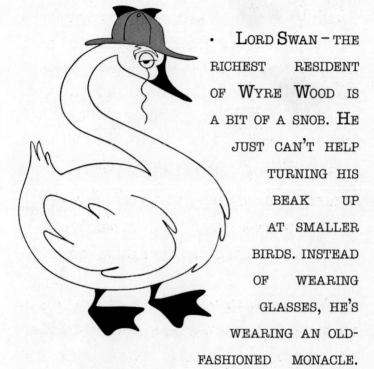

LORD SWAN – THE RICHEST RESIDENT OF WYRE WOOD IS A BIT OF A SNOB. HE JUST CAN'T HELP TURNING HIS BEAK UP AT SMALLER BIRDS. INSTEAD OF WEARING GLASSES, HE'S WEARING AN OLD-FASHIONED MONACLE. I EXPECT IT COMES IN HANDY FOR LOOKING DOWN ON THE FLOCKS OF FEATHERED RIFF-RAFF.

A NOTE FROM THE AUTHOR...

Some of you may have visited a wood, to have a picnic, play games, ride bikes or walk in the sunshine. But have you ever thought about what the animals get up to once you have left? Have you ever wondered if the birds really do just sit in trees all day? And what do you suppose they get up to at night?

Well, in the county of Featherfordshire, there is a small town called Sunnyport. The town nestles between the Lickey Hills and the River Ayt. It looks like a very ordinary town in a very ordinary county – but if you look closely, it has a secret...

THE LOCATION:

Wyre Wood

Entrance

Parking

Playground

Squirrel Lodge

East Oak

The Magpies

The Krows

Visitors' Centre

West Wood

Old Oak Stump

East Wood

Hawkbatch Market

Open Air Theatre

Cycle Path

Post Office

Traders' Cafe

Swans

Police Station

Birch Comprehensive School

N
W　E
S

River Ayt

CHAPTER ONE:
NOISES IN THE NIGHT

Nestling between the beautiful river Ayt and the busy town of Sunnyport sits Wyre Wood. In the olden days, rich lords and ladies used to hunt deer in the wood. But now it sits quietly; welcoming Sunday visitors and dog walkers. Full of conifers, oaks, silver birches (and a whole forest of other types of tree that I do not have time to mention) this is not a large wood – but it is a very, very special wood.

Lots of animals live here. Foxes, rabbits, squirrels and stoats. But it is the birds, who rule the wood!

You might not see them, but they are there; and they are like no other birds you'll ever see. They behave, dress and live life just like you do. There are good birds, bad birds, young and old birds. They have shops and homes and schools – they even have their own police force...

Winter had already started to squeeze its icy fingers around the trees. It was a freezing night and a thick fog hung in the air, dripping over the bare branches. The birds shivered, but not because of the cold. This was a special night for the bird life of Wyre Wood. The invitations had gone out weeks ago. Now all the richest and most powerful birds (including some of the wood's worst villains) were flocking to its eastern corner for a very special evening.

Every year in the middle of winter, all the birds got ready for an event that had become 'infamous' (that's when something is famous for being bad!) Although it was a special night, it wasn't a night for fun. It was a night when you had to pretend to be enjoying yourself – even if you weren't. A bit like when you visit your auntie's house and she asks if you'd like extra prawns on your omelette.

Bright lights filled the night sky as hundreds of birds circled over the East Oak.

Two enormous buzzards called Brian and Derek were standing guard. They kept busy by flexing their wings and picking at their black and broken beaks with their crooked claws. This pair of feathered thugs would work for anyone with deep enough pockets. Tonight they were guarding the entrance for The Krows. A sign over the door read:

MAGPIES KEEP OUT!

The Magpies were a rival gang and the Krows' sworn enemies. They were definitely NOT invited tonight.

'Hurry up!' squawked Brian, as the guests hopped through the entrance.

When the last few birds were inside the hollow oak, the buzzard bouncers shut the door with a bang.

After a few minutes, nothing could be heard from inside the tree except beautiful music. Tomorrow it was the birthday of one of the oldest residents of Wyre Wood, and Luciano Megawarble – the world-famous nightingale – had flown in specially to give one of his performances.

As he sang a melody from an opera by Ludwig von Goshawk, the buzzards stood side-by-side, wings crossed and eyes alert making sure that the door stayed closed until the concert was over.

But gentle music was not the only sound coming from inside the tree. A loud argument was also going on. None of the guests had the nerve to do anything but sit still with their wings crossed and carry on listening to the singing. The shouting was coming from two black crows with nasty eyes and even nastier hearts.

'Do this right or else! You stupid chavvinch!' growled one of the crows as he pushed something into a small bird's terrified claw.

'Bbbbbbbut…!' stuttered the shaking chaffinch.

'No buts, bird! Just do as you are told!' said the second crow.

Everyone in Wyre Wood knew the voices of the two bullies. They were Tommy and Terry – the Krow Twins!

CHAPTER TWO:
THE BIRD POLICE

Detective Inspector George Hoot swooped into his office in Wyre Wood police station. The old tawny owl headed straight for his desk, which was covered with reports he'd never read. Jane, a small sparrow in charge of the police station was already making a hot drink for Hoot.

'Good morning, Jane.'

Hoot dropped into his usual seat close to the fire, stretched his wings and tried to get the cold out of his feathers. 'What should I know about today, then?'

'Well, the magpies have complained about all the noise coming from the East Oak last night. They claim that one of their nests was vandalised,' answered Jane. 'But other than that we had a really quiet night, sir.'

Jane had been greeted with much less paperwork than usual when she opened up the station that morning. Saturday night in the wood usually brought a few birds who had drunk too much berry juice. But last night had been unusually calm, thanks to so many of the trouble-makers being busy at the Krows' concert.

'File the magpies' complaint in the usual place, Jane,' sighed Hoot.

The usual place for complaints from the magpies was the bin! As far as Hoot was concerned, the two gangs were as bad as each other.

'Last night's concert made the morning edition of *The Squirrel Times*, sir,' added Jane, as she handed Hoot his copy of the newspaper.

'Apparently most of the audience couldn't see a thing thanks to Mother Krow's ridiculous hat! It was big enough to be seen from space! That old bird has no fashion sense – she sticks out like a sliced loaf in a duck pond.'

Hoot snorted. As the ageing detective tucked into his morning seed cake, dropping crumbs all over his feathers, the office door swung open and a small starling fluttered in.

'Good morning! I'm looking for Detective

Hoot,' said the police's newest officer, Bird Constable Florisa Starling.

Starling stood to attention and felt every bit as nervous as she looked. This was her first day in the Wyre Wood police force.

'That's Detective Inspector Hoot, to you,' said the owl as he slowly raised his huge eyes from the newspaper and looked the newcomer up and down. 'And you are?'

'Bird Constable Florisa Starling, sir! The Academy sent me.' Starling was trying to sound braver than she felt.

'The 'Academy' eh?' scoffed Hoot. 'Well that counts for nothing here! Experience is the only thing that matters. You are here to learn – understand?'

'Yes, sir!' replied Starling. She'd fought hard to get into the Bird Police Academy, and come top of her class – but she wasn't about to get into an argument with her boss on her first day.

As Hoot's great big eyes took in Starling's uniform, he began to beat his wings in anger.

'We need to start with some basics Starling. In my day, uniforms were treated with respect,' boomed Hoot.

'Sorry sir?' said Florisa.

'Why are you covered in glitter Starling!'

'I thought...,' began Florisa, but she quickly closed her beak when she saw Hoot's face.

'Thought?' screeched Hoot. 'I wasn't taught to think when I was a new recruit.'

But before Hoot could start his speech about following the dress code (which did not include decorating your police uniform with glitter), Jane burst into the office.

'Inspector Hoot, there's a message for you – it's just come in.'

'What is it?' demanded Hoot snapping his eyes up from Starling's glittery feet.

'Sir, Lord Swan has had a priceless painting stolen! He wants to know what you are going to do about it.'

'Right, I'm on the case,' said Hoot hopping out of his chair and flying towards the station door. 'Starling, come with me to the river. And you can get rid of that ridiculous glitter on the way!'

CHAPTER THREE:
LORD SWAN

The river Ayt was some distance away from the police station and Starling had to work hard to keep up with Hoot. For an old owl he was a very fast flapper.

Today the river wasn't looking its best. In deep winter, its edges always froze, hiding a dangerous current that ran down the middle. Many a young bird, after a night's partying, had gone for a bath and ended up being swept away.

Hoot and Starling swooped down.

'Be careful where you land,' warned Hoot. 'This is a dangerous area. I know you've passed your police swimming test – but these are nasty waters. Get caught in the flow and we might never see you again!'

As the two Bird Officers were talking, a proud swan slowly started to swim over. It was Lord Swan, the richest resident of the river. Eventually, he reached the bank and slowly waddled towards the officers – stretching his enormous wings to their full size and giving them a little shake.

'Good afternoon, my Lord,' said Hoot, bowing low and nudging Florisa to do the same.

'Have you found my painting yet?' flapped Lord Swan, peering down his yellow and black bill.

'We've only just arrived, sir,' Hoot muttered. 'But we'll do everything we can.'

'Well, get to it – what are you waiting for? The thief has left his filthy prints all over my beautiful riverbank!' honked the swan. And with that he turned on his huge webbed feet and marched back to the water.

'I was taught all the latest ways of solving crimes at the academy, sir,' said Florisa. 'Shall I dust for bird prints?'

'You won't need your daft ideas here my girl. Just watch and learn,' said Hoot, hopping over to inspect the area.

Next to a willow tree they saw a large

patch of mud covered in bird prints. The cold night had frozen them solid.

'Do you want me to start a wing-tip search?' asked Starling.

'A wing-tip search? What are you talking about?' laughed Hoot. 'Use your eyes. That's all a police officer needs. What do you see?'

'Well. There are lots of bird prints...' began Florisa.

'Those aren't just any bird prints Starling, they are obviously chaffinch tracks!' cried Hoot rolling his eyes. 'And there is only one chaffinch in this wood who could be mixed up in something like this. I know exactly where to find him – and his evil bosses!'

'Are you absolutely sure they're chaffinch

tracks, sir?' asked Florisa. She knew there was something very strange about these mysterious prints, but she couldn't quite put her wing on it.

'I know a chaffinch footprint when I see one!' boomed Hoot.

'I'm not so sure, sir,' said Florisa quietly.

'You don't have to be sure Starling. I am sure and that is all you need to know. We are going to pay a visit to the Krow Twins. It's about time you met the two villains who think they run this wood.'

'I just need to take some photographs of these prints sir, before it gets dark, and get them off to the lab,' said Starling.

Scrambling around in her jacket for her camera, Starling didn't notice the angry look on Hoot's face.

'Fine! You stay here and play with your camera. I'll get on with the real police work, shall I?' said Hoot as he took off.

Circling back over Starling's head, he cried: 'Meet me at the East Oak Tree when you're done! And be quick about it!'

CHAPTER FOUR:
A 'SPECIAL' GIFT

The East Oak was a hive of activity. Last night's concert was only the beginning of the celebrations. Tonight was the main event – Mother Krow's birthday party.

The Krows' parties were famously grand. On one side of the dance floor, some tree stumps were piled high with food. Seed cake, nuts, dried berries, mouse pies, rat-flavoured biscuits, rabbit paté, juicy maggots, beetles, and worms of assorted sizes had been laid out on evergreen leaves. But no one had started to enjoy the feast yet, the Krows had not given their guests permission to eat.

Many of the birds were perched next to a gnarled stump, where a particularly nasty-looking jackdaw with a muddy beak was serving berry juice. Bits of wood, tree bark and dead spiders floated in the drinks, but no one seemed to mind. It just made it tastier!

As the lights flashed on the dance floor, a truly evil-looking mob of birds could be seen trying to dance. They had scarred beaks, missing feathers, broken wings and chipped claws. This rag-tag crew were The Krows' younger cousins – nicknamed 'The Hoodies' thanks to their black heads. They'd travelled to the Wood especially for the party.

Sat on a bench made from twigs and winter leaves, watching the dancing, was old Mother Krow. To her left stood a table bending under the weight of presents – from bottles of vintage berry juice to feather jewellery, no expense had been spared.

A long line of nervous birds moved slowly past. One at a time, each bird offered Mother Krow their gift and card. At the front of the line was an old goldfinch.

'Happy Birthday Matilda,' he chirped. 'So how old are you this year?'

The birds waiting behind him couldn't believe their ears. They hopped back and held their breath, expecting something horrible to happen. Instead, a smile slowly appeared over Mother Krow's face.

'That is not a question to ask a lady, Leonardo Da Finchi,' she answered. 'All I'll say is that my two boys keep me feeling young.' Mother Krow glanced lovingly over at her 'boys'.

'Mind your manners, Da Finchi,' squawked Tommy Krow. 'You better watch your beak from now on.'

'Yeah, shut your worm hole,' added Terry.

'Now now boys,' said Mother Krow, 'Leonardo is an old friend of mine.'

'I know!' said Tommy under his breath. The Krow brothers had always hated Da Finchi. The boys thought he was far too friendly with their Mum.

Da Finchi smiled.

'Look, I've brought you a very special present, Matilda. I have painted you a picture.'

He dipped his wing towards a painting which was leaning against the table.

Leonardo Da Finchi was Wyre Wood's leading artist. All the rich birds just HAD to have one of his paintings. Little did they know, Leonardo was also a master forger. He'd paint fake versions of famous pictures by great artists. Then the Krows would sell them on to art collectors who thought they were buying the real thing. It was against the law to sell a fake, but it was worth a fortune.

'What do you think, boys?' asked Mother Krow, proud of her new painting.

Tommy stared at the picture. This was definitely not one of Da Finchi's better works of "art".

Covered in random shapes and weird blobs of colour, you could just make out a big rectangle that might possibly be the East Oak tree.

It was a style called 'modern art' but Tommy reckoned that a baby bird could do better. There were crazy shapes and lopsided splotches of brown paint all over the place.

'It's lovely, Mum,' said Tommy, not wanting to upset his mother.

'Yeah - a real masterpiece,' laughed Terry sarcastically.

'Don't you try to be funny with me!' snapped his mother. The room fell silent. All eyes were now on old Mother Krow who was glaring at her son.

Tommy gawped. Terry began to fidget and quickly looked down at his clawed feet, trying to avoid his mother's angry stare.

But before he could open his beak to beg for her forgiveness, there was a loud shout from the buzzard bouncers. Two unexpected visitors came swooping into the party and landed smack in the middle of the dance floor.

CHAPTER FIVE:
A PARTY
INTERRUPTED...

When Hoot and Starling crashed into the scene, all the guests stepped back and followed the police officers with worried eyes. The music stopped and everyone stood and waited. Hoot hopped over to where Mother Krow was sitting, followed by a nervous Starling, who had never been to a criminal's party before.

'Good evening Mother Krow and happy birthday,' said Hoot, ignoring the two Krow brothers moving towards him. As Hoot got closer to M o t h e r K r o w, her sons jumped to her side.

'What do you want, copper?' demanded Tommy. Although he wouldn't admit it, he'd never been so pleased to see a police officer in his life. It had got him off the hook for being rude about his mother's new painting.

'That's Detective Inspector Hoot to you, Krow. Now where's that pet chaffinch of yours?'

'Dwayne's not here,' said Terry, twisting his vicious beak into a grin.

Hoot looked around. There was no sign of Dwayne but something else caught his eye.

'Like collecting paintings, do you boys? Starting a gallery, are you? What do you know about the art theft at Lord Swan's place last night?'

The Krows tried to look surprised.

'A theft? That's terrible,' said Tommy pretending to be concerned.

'Oh dear oh dear! What is this wood coming to?' sniggered Terry.

Hoot and Starling moved over to Da Finchi's present. Tommy and Terry Krow glared at them.

'What are those strange marks at the

bottom of this picture?' asked Starling. Florisa had noticed that the painting had a line of odd-looking bird prints at the bottom.

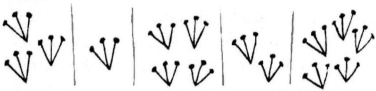

'Good question,' said Hoot.

'That's my signature. All great artists sign their work,' said Da Finchi proudly.

Starling pulled a camera out of her jacket pocket and started taking pictures. Da Finchi was furious.

'You can't do that! How dare you photograph my work?!' he cried.

Da Finchi reached over to grab the camera but Starling pulled it away just in time.

'What's wrong Da Finchi?' said Hoot. 'Got something to hide?''

Da Finchi fluttered off in a hurry and landed behind Mother Krow, who was now looking confused. Hoot had long suspected that Da Finchi not only painted his own pictures but also did some forgery on the side. He was obviously guilty about something.

'You'd better come back to the station with me and answer some questions.'

Da Finchi was in no mood to leave the party. He glared at Hoot.

'I'm not going anywhere. If you want me to come to the police station, then arrest me!' he cried.

'I only want a little help with my enquiries – but we could try police harassment if you prefer!' answered Hoot, stretching his talons. It had been a long day and the old owl was getting fed up with this nonsense.

'No need to argue, Inspector,' interrupted Mother Krow, putting a wing on Da Finchi's shoulder. 'Leonardo will be happy to help you with your enquiries, after my party has finished.'

'Fine! I'll see you tomorrow Da Finchi. Enjoy the rest of your party, Matilda,' said Hoot. Then he nodded at Starling, and the two officers took flight.

41

CHAPTER SIX:
THE STRANGE
SIGNATURE

On their way back to the station, Hoot and Starling flew over Birch Comprehensive. Its great iron gates had seen better days. Starling went to the school when she was a chick and even then it had a reputation for being tough. However, now she had other things on her mind.

'Sir, why does an artist like Da Finchi need to sign his paintings with strange patterns of prints?' asked Starling.

But Hoot had spotted some young birds about to paint graffiti on the school wall.

'Oi, you lot – what do you think you're doing?' cried Hoot, swooping down.

'What do you want, you daft old buzzard?' answered one of the cheekier birds.

'I'm not too old to give you a flying lesson – with my claws against your tail feathers!' hissed Hoot, swooping lower to give the birds a scare. 'I know you Karl. Didn't I catch you playing conkers with dead mice

42

last year? Get back home now.' Hoot sighed and flew back up to Starling.

Florisa was still thinking about Da Finchi.

'Why doesn't he do a normal signature? Just leave one print at the bottom of his paintings?' she asked.

'What?' snapped Hoot, finally listening to Starling. 'I don't care how that old crook signs his daft pictures. Probably thinks he's River Banksy or something. Anyway, we need to find Dwayne the chaffinch. He might be able to explain those mysterious prints by the river at Lord Swan's place.'

They searched for Dwayne but there was no sign of him anywhere so the two officers flew back to the police station. They were glad to get back to the warmth of Hoot's office. But before they had time to find a perch, Jane fluttered in with the lab results.

'Sir, the prints left by the riverbank don't belong to a chaffinch. They were made by a goldfinch!'

'Are you sure, Jane?' gasped Hoot.

He wasn't going to admit that he had been wrong in a hurry.

'Yes, sir, definitely goldfinch prints, sir.'

'Well then, it's simple…' cried Hoot, already on his way out of the office. 'There's only one goldfinch in these woods! I'm off to bring Da Finchi in. No wonder he didn't want to talk!'

'But it's the middle of the night, sir!' said Starling.

'Police work is a 24-hour job, Starling,' answered Hoot. 'Perhaps he's at the party.'

'At this hour Sir?' asked Starling.

They searched and searched, but Da Finchi was nowhere to be found. Every dark corner, hidden tree stump and nightclub nest was investigated. Owls are used to staying up all night and Hoot enjoyed working under the cover of darkness. Poor Starling, however, was finding out that having an owl for a boss meant long nights full of work and no time for supper.

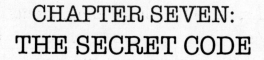

CHAPTER SEVEN:
THE SECRET CODE

The next morning, Starling dragged her tired feathers back into the police station, still thinking about the strange marks that Da Finchi used to sign his paintings.

She decided to go and see Jane in the lab. It was full of dusty equipment, most of it in boxes still waiting to be opened. Police Headquarters kept sending them new gadgets, but Hoot refused to even think about using them. The ancient owl liked old-fashioned policing. He believed that flying about listening and talking to witnesses was all it took to solve a case.

Jane loved the peace and quiet in the lab, away from Hoot's screeching orders. It was the one place that Hoot never came.

Perched in a snug corner, Jane was reading some papers when Starling appeared.

'Morning Florisa,' twittered Jane, surprised to see anyone in the lab. 'Did you manage to get any sleep last night?'

'Not much,' answered Florisa, rubbing her

tired eyes and looking for a place to perch. 'Does DCI Hoot ever get tired?'

'I think he does dear, but he won't ever show it,' replied Jane. The sparrow had worked with Hoot for a very long time and she knew he was a tough old bird.

'Have some seed cake and sit down. I made it fresh yesterday.'

Jane passed Florisa some cake and the young starling pecked at it thoughtfully.

'Have you printed out the snaps I took at Mother Krow's party?' asked Florisa through a beak full of cake. The room felt warm and cosy, it was all Starling could do to keep her eyes open after her long night looking for Da Finchi.

'Yes, dear, here they are.'

Jane passed the pictures over to Starling who spread them out on the desk.

'Here are the ones you took of Da Finchi's 'masterpiece' at Ma Krow's party. I don't know what people see in his paintings – this one is awful! Is that square thing supposed to be the East Oak? '

Florisa giggled.

'Da Finchi must be losing his touch, trying

to do all this modern art,' said Jane. 'His old ones were quite good you know. We've even got one here in the office.'

'You're joking!' gasped a shocked Starling. 'Surely Hoot wouldn't allow that?'

'Well, Da Finchi made a lot of fuss about giving a painting to the old police commissioner when he retired. Hoot uses it to keep the back door open in the summer!' chuckled Jane.

Perched side by side, they examined the pictures.

'There's something really odd about the prints we found at Lord Swan's,' mumbled Florisa, thinking out loud. 'I still don't understand why Da Finchi would sign his painting in such an unusual way.'

'Looks like a code to me,' said Jane, waving her wing at the Da Finchi's strange signature.

'What?' cried Florisa, suddenly feeling wide awake.

'Many of the old artists left secret codes in their paintings. It's a well known fact,' continued Jane not realising the importance of what she'd just said.

'A code! That's it. You are brilliant, Jane! But what does it mean?' asked Starling, almost dropping her cake.

'That's the thing about codes, dear,' said Jane. 'They're supposed to be secret.'

'Where's Hoot? I must tell him about this immediately!' squawked Starling.

'I think he's at the market, dear,' answered Jane. But before she had time to finish her sentence, Starling was already taking off out of the door.

CHAPTER EIGHT:
A DANGEROUS
DECISION

Every Monday, Wyre Wood held a market at Hawkbatch. Lots of birds would go there to shop. Stalls of all kinds stood side-by-side. Some were covered with roofs made of twigs tied together to keep the rain off, while others were nothing more than old tree stumps turned into tables. The air was filled with chatter as the stall holders cried out to the passing crowd.

There was nothing that couldn't be bought at Hawkbatch. The noise from the market could be heard in every corner of the wood and the smell of mice kebabs, roasted seeds and berry juice filled the air.

At the market café, Starling found Hoot. Last night, he'd carried on looking for Da Finchi long after Starling had gone back to her nest. Now it was morning, and he was feeling sleepy.

Starling couldn't wait to tell Hoot about

Jane's idea. But when he heard about the code, the owl rolled his large round eyes.

'What in Tweet's name are you going on about, Starling? Has lack of sleep fried your brain? I'm not interested in signatures. We need basic police work, Starling. Concentrate on the evidence!'

But Starling WAS concentrating on the evidence. However, she could tell that Hoot wasn't in the mood to listen. A code hidden in the signature on a painting was too far-fetched for the old owl to accept.

As Hoot turned to order a berry juice, the café door flew open and a scruffy-looking chaffinch came fluttering in. He looked like he hadn't slept for days. It was Dwayne.

'Oi, chavvinch, I want a word with you!' boomed Hoot, shoving past a queue of traders to get to the terrified bird.

As Hoot swooped towards Dwayne, Starling caught a glimpse of a golden wing out of the corner of her eye.

'It's Da Finchi!' she called. As Hoot turned to see what was happening, Dwayne saw his chance to escape. He swooped off out of the door but crashed straight into a stall, twittering curses as it toppled over.

'Watch it, mate!' shouted the owner. His carefully piled berries were scattered all over the ground. 'You've squashed my display!!'

CLANK!

Something dropped from Dwayne's pocket as he picked himself up; it was a funny looking object shaped like a claw.

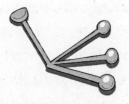

Dwayne quickly scooped it up and then flew off in a tremendous hurry. Starling, who had seen everything, took off in pursuit.

'After him Starling!' screeched Hoot as Florisa disappeared into the morning fog.

Spitting mad, Hoot turned towards Da Finchi. 'All right Da Finchi. You're coming with me!' he said.

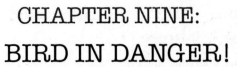

CHAPTER NINE:
BIRD IN DANGER!

The morning mist got thicker as Starling raced after Dwayne. Although she'd been trained to chase criminals through trees at high speeds, the wood looked different when it was locked in a blanket of fog. Swooping around the icy branches, Starling was slowly catching up with Dwayne. The flashes of white on his wings and tail feathers made the chaffinch an easy bird to follow. But just as she thought she could force Dwayne to land, she spotted two shadows on either side of her. With the flap of battle-scarred wings, two buzzards had appeared. Soon they were closing in on Florisa. The young starling didn't stand a chance against these brutes.

'You're under arrest, Dwayne!' called Florisa, trying to sound brave, 'You have the right to remain silent…'

But before Starling could finish, the two burly buzzards flew at her, flicked their huge dark wings and sent her crashing to

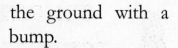

the ground with a bump.

'You ain't arresting no one, little birdy!' laughed one of the buzzards, bobbing his ugly head up and down.

Using her wings to push herself up from the cold ground, Starling tried to look confident.

'Feeling brave are you, Dwayne? Now you've got your thugs to help you?'

The buzzards landed on top of Florisa. Before she had a chance to do anything, one of them grabbed her tail and was holding her tight.

Dwayne hopped slowly over to her, flexed his wings and leaned in close.

'Go on then birdy ... arrest me!' he laughed. 'Oh, I'm sorry – you can't! You should have left well alone, little Starling!'

CHAPTER TEN:
QUESTION TIME

Back at the police station, Hoot had put Da Finchi into a holding nest. Criminal birds of all shapes and sizes knew these nests to be dark and miserable places. A tiny perch had been placed in the middle of the nest, and Hoot stood to one side staring at his prisoner.

'Where were you on Saturday night?' he demanded.

'Watching Luciano Megawarble singing at Mother Krow's concert. Lovely show, but only for a very select audience, as you'd know – if you had been invited,' sneered Da Finchi.

'What makes you think I'd want to waste my evening with you and the Krows?' snapped Hoot. 'Where were you AFTER the concert?' he demanded, his voice getting louder.

'I was in my workshop,' said Da Finchi.

'Where exactly is that? Anywhere near

Lord Swan's place?' asked Hoot.

'I know my rights. I don't have to say anything unless I have been arrested!' replied Da Finchi, looking down his beak at the inspector.

'All right then, have it your way. Leonardo Da Finchi, I'm arresting you on suspicion of the theft of...' but before Hoot could continue, Da Finchi raised a wing.

'Wait! There's no need to be hasty. The location of my workshop is a secret! But it's nowhere near Lord Swan's house,' said Leonardo.

'Give me one good reason why I shouldn't arrest you Da Finchi? We found goldfinch prints all over the crime scene.'

'I can prove I was in my workshop – my girlfriend was with me!' he twittered.

Hoot rolled his eyes.

'Well, we'll see about that, won't we,' replied Hoot. 'You can go, for now. But I'm going to have a little word with your girlfriend, and if your story doesn't stand up, you're going to be spending a lot of time in a cage!'

CHAPTER ELEVEN: THE SECRET WORKSHOP

Leonardo Da Finchi took off out of Wyre Wood police station as though his tail feathers were on fire. Meanwhile, Hoot hopped out into the hallway, where he bumped into a worried-looking Jane.

'Have you heard from Starling, sir? She hasn't called in for hours,' said the old sparrow.

The owl gave her a piercing stare.

'Never mind Starling! We need to follow Da Finchi. That old crook is scared – and I want to know why.'

Hoot flew out of the station, keeping Da Finchi in sight, with Jane close behind.

The pair struggled to keep up with Da Finchi, but at last they spotted his yellow wings in the distance.

They would have caught up with him if it wasn't for a group of young birds who got in their way. They were learning to fly, and going very slowly. Seeing the two police officers made them even more nervous. The last thing these learners wanted was a speeding ticket.

Hoot peered through the flock, trying to keep Da Finchi in sight. At last, he saw the goldfinch land and disappear into some brambles. Swooping down, the clever old owl hopped after him.

'Look sir,' whispered Jane excitedly, waving her wing towards the ground. 'Goldfinch tracks!'

They were leading into the thorny thicket.

Hoot peered closely at the bird prints, and as his huge round eyes followed the trail he couldn't believe it. He spotted a tiny oak door with a shiny keypad on it, just visible through the bramble branches.

'Well, well, well, what do we have here then?' muttered Hoot.

'It must be Da Finchi's secret workshop,' replied Jane, hurrying over to the door.

She poked her beak closer to the metal keypad to get a better look. 'But how in Tweet's name are we going to get inside?'

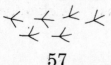

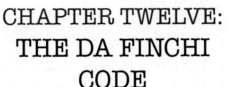

CHAPTER TWELVE:
THE DA FINCHI CODE

Both birds examined the keypad, prodding it carefully with their wing tips. It had numbers on it:

1   2   3

4   5   6

7   8   9

'Well, if I know that tricky old goldfinch, he's trying to be clever,' said Hoot as he rubbed his big eyes with his wing. Even owls get tired sometimes.

Jane's eyes lit up. Like Starling, she'd also been thinking about the strange marks at the bottom of Da Finchi's painting. Now it all suddenly made sense.

'Look at these photos that Starling took, sir!' she said taking out some pictures from her jacket. Hoot gave her a puzzled look.

'What have you got in mind, Jane?' he asked. Jane didn't answer. She began to enter numbers into the keypad and waited in excitement for the click of a lock – but nothing happened.

'Stand back!' screeched Hoot. 'What we need now is a bit of police force!' He hopped back from the door, preparing to fly straight at it.

'Hang on, sir. We want to surprise him, don't we? I'll explain. Now, look at the signature on that awful modern painting that Da Finchi gave to Mother Krow. There's three, one, four, two and five bird prints all in little groups.'

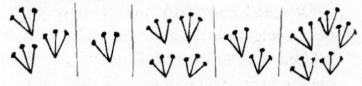

Hoot stared at Jane. 'And?' he blustered.

'Well, I'll try again. I'll just enter the numbers: 3, 1, 4, 2 and 5 into the keypad...' said Jane.

'Go on then! Get on with it!' cried Hoot.

Jane's face fell. Again, nothing happened.

'It didn't work!' moaned Jane. 'Sorry Sir, I was sure I'd cracked it.'

'Hang on a minute,' said Hoot. 'Last year we found those messages that Da Finchi was sending to the Krows. We couldn't understand them. Remember?'

'Not really, sir. Why?'

'Well, Headquarters eventually worked out that he was writing the messages backwards. It's called 'mirror writing' because you can only read the message when you look at it in a mirror.'

'Shall I fly off and get a mirror Sir?' chirped Jane, sounding confused.

'No need!' boomed Hoot. 'Just try the numbers backwards.'

'Good idea Sir,' said Jane.

'Trust me,' said Hoot. 'It's just the kind of trick Da Finchi would try.'

Jane dutifully keyed in all of the numbers but in reverse order this time. She used the very tips of her wings to enter: 5, 2, 4, 1 and 3 into the keypad...

CLICK!

The little door swung open.

'We've done it!' screeched Hoot in triumph. 'We've cracked Da Finchi's secret code!'

CHAPTER THIRTEEN: A SECRET REVEALED

Inside, the space was dimly lit with half-melted candles dripping onto the floor. Strange shadows flickered across the walls and cobwebs full of dead flies dangled from every corner. Da Finchi's workshop seemed to go on and on for miles under the wood. It smelled old and dusty but it was surprisingly warm. Hoot and Jane soon came upon a huge chimney with a fire flickering in the grate. Reflections danced on the mirrors and glass cabinets that lined the walls.

The floor was covered with paint pots of every colour imaginable. Strewn amongst the pots were brushes: fat, thin, short and long. Canvases of all shapes and sizes were scattered about the place. Some of them were half-finished, some were complete and others were hidden under ripped pieces of cloth.

'Da Finchi. We know you're in here!' cried

Hoot, swooping towards a dark corner with Jane not far behind.

CRASH!

'Suffering seagulls!' screeched Hoot. He'd flown straight into Da Finchi, who was now lying in a heap on the floor. Next to the goldfinch was a large bundle wrapped in cloth.

Wasting no time, Hoot carefully ripped the cloth open with one of his talons.

'Cross-eyed cormorants! What have we here?' said Hoot. In his claw was a beautiful painting. It was 'The Golden Sunflowers,' by the famous artist Vincent van Chough. The painting was magnificent – its orange and yellow colours shone in the dim candlelight. This was not one of Da Finchi's 'masterpieces'. This was the stolen painting belonging to Lord Swan!

'That's not mine,' Da Finchi pleaded.

'Obviously not,' said Hoot. 'It's far too good to be one of your paintings. It belongs to Lord Swan.' Hoot was enjoying every minute of this.

'It's nothing to do with me, I tell you!' said Da Finchi, in a panic. 'Somebody's trying to frame me.'

'Oh very funny! "Frame" you! Is that your idea of a joke?' sneered Hoot.

'I'm serious Inspector, someone has left that picture here to make me look guilty.'

Hoot stared at the goldfinch. There was something about the way Da Finchi was acting, he sounded too scared to be lying.

'Who'd do a thing like that, I wonder?' whispered Hoot.

'Who do you think? The Krows, of course! They've always hated me.'

Da Finchi was hopping from claw to claw, nearly in tears. He'd tricked so many people over the years with his forged paintings and got away with it. The thought of spending the next ten years of his life behind bars for a crime he hadn't committed was more than he could stand.

'Jane,' said Hoot, 'Take this one back to the station and throw him into a holding nest. I'm going after the Krows!'

'Yes, Sir. But what about Bird Constable Starling? She's been gone for ages.'

With Lord Swan's precious painting recovered, Hoot finally remembered that Florisa was missing. At last, the old owl started to looked worried.

'Send for The Sparrowhawk Squad,' cried Hoot. 'Tell them to search the wood and then meet me at the East Oak.'

And with that, DCI Hoot took off, whilst Jane escorted a silent and scared Da Finchi back to the station. The artist was feeling very sorry for himself indeed.

CHAPTER FOURTEEN: THE KROWS' NEST!

As night gripped the wood, DCI Hoot raced over to the East Oak as fast as his old wings could carry him. With all the party decorations gone, the lower branches of the tree cast shadows across the ground like a witch's fingers. Mistletoe hung in its highest branches, making the tree look like it was wearing a strange bushy hat.

The two bullying buzzards, Brian and Derek, were perched on one of the tree's biggest branches. As soon as they saw Hoot coming, they swooped down. The pair had been having a dull night, and this was a chance for some excitement! They flew at the police officer, spreading their wings in massive 'V' shapes and squawking in anger.

But as the brainless buzzards swooped down, Hoot changed direction and they flew into each other with a loud crash.

Ignoring their curses, Hoot headed for the massive trunk of the East Oak.

The great tree had stood for more than a hundred years. As the seasons came and went, cracks had appeared in its base. Over time, the cracks got bigger and formed tunnels. A less-experienced bird could easily get lost in them and never be seen again, but Hoot had been in the tree many times over the years. He knew that this was the only place to find the Krows. Ripping through strands of ivy, Hoot heard the sound of three familiar voices.

'You stupid chavvinch! You've got a lot of front, bringing that starling here,' said Tommy.

'Sorry, boss, but she was chasing me. I don't think she saw me drop the claw though,' squeaked a terrified Dwayne.

'If you've brought the law down on us, you'd better start saying your prayers!' croaked Terry Krow in a rage.

'Get praying then, Dwayne,' said Hoot, hopping out of the shadows. 'But before you do that, you can start singing. Why would two crows and a chaffinch want to steal Lord Swan's painting and stash it in Da Finchi's secret workshop?'

Dwayne said nothing. One look from Tommy was enough to make him keep his beak shut.

Terry Krow ruffled his great black wings and laughed nervously. Hoot shook his head. He might not be the most famous detective in the country, but you didn't have to be Hercule Parrot to see that the Krow twins were hiding something.

The silence was broken by a thump, followed by a muffled moan. Hoot snapped his huge eyes over to where the noise was coming from. He spotted something sticking out from under a dirty old sheet. But dirt wasn't the only thing he could see – there was glitter everywhere.

'Starling!' cried Hoot, tugging at the sheet with his beak. As it started to come loose, Starling flapped and struggled. The rope that Dwayne had tied her up with was strong, but Hoot's sharp talons cut through it easily. With feathers flying and a lot of spluttering, Starling finally dragged herself free.

CHAPTER FIFTEEN:
A MYSTERY SOLVED

'Thanks, sir,' said Starling. Wobbling about like a baby bird, she hopped closer to Hoot. She was still more than a bit shaken from her run in with the buzzards.

'Make Dwayne show you what he has got in his jacket, sir,' shouted Starling.

'You heard the officer. Got something to show me have you?' demanded Hoot.

Tommy Krow groaned.

'Worried about something, Tommy?' laughed Hoot.

A terrified Dwayne looked over to Tommy – and then back at Hoot.

'I ain't got nuffin' in my jacket, 'cept a few dried berries me ma gave me.'

On hearing this, Hoot flew into a terrible rage. Swooping at Dwayne, he grabbed the chaffinch's jacket, ripped it open and pulled out a mysterious claw-shaped object.

'Recognise that, Dwayne?' Starling squawked from where she was sitting. 'It's a fake claw.

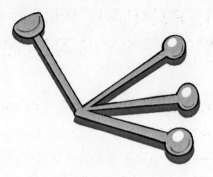

Someone used it to leave false goldfinch prints at Lord Swan's place.'

Turning to Hoot, Starling continued: 'They wanted to make it look as if Da Finchi had stolen the painting, sir.'

'Well done copper – you've got the villain right there. My brother and I are ashamed to call that chavvinch our friend!' said Tommy. Hoot raised himself to his full height and faced up to Tommy Krow.

'Ashamed, eh?' said Hoot. 'Well, you and your evil brother are under arrest as well. Dwayne's not clever enough to do all this on his own; and I have got a stolen painting back at the station. I bet it has your prints all over it.'

Tommy and Terry were already heading for the door. They raced back down the dark tunnel and as they were scrabbling out through the tree trunk, four strapping sparrowhawks appeared.

CRASH!

The Krows didn't know what had hit them. The Sparrowhawk Patrol Squad had arrived just in time. As the hawks pinned the villains' wings behind their backs, Tommy and Terry pecked and scratched with all their might. But it was no good. The only place they were going was a holding nest back at the police station.

'Got 'em, sir!' squawked Sid, the leader of the Squad.

As Hoot emerged from the tree trunk, dragging a terrified Dwayne behind him, Florisa limped out happy to be breathing the fresh air again.

'All right, Sid? Cuff them and get them back to the station,' said Hoot proudly.

'You've got nothing on us, owl!' screeched Tommy, as Sid and the rest of the squad prepared to fly off with the prisoners.

'Hang on, Sid,' said Hoot.

He swooped straight over to Tommy, twisted the bird around so he could stare straight into his dark eyes and laughed.

'I've waited a long time for this, Krow. Your old ma can't save you now! I bet you a month's supply of seed cake that Dwayne will tell us everything before the day has ended!'

CHAPTER SIXTEEN:
THE TRIAL

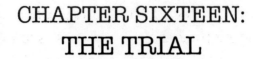

The birds of Wyre Wood had been talking about the arrest of the Krow twins for weeks. Today, a large flock had gathered outside the court. They'd been waiting all morning to hear the result of the greatest trial the wood had ever seen. Just as the crowd was starting to think about lunch, the huge oak doors of the court tree burst open and an angry owl marched out.

'Can you believe it?' spat Hoot. The old owl was moving so fast that Jane had to flap hard to keep up with him.

'Hoot! Hoot!!' A crowd of cuckoo news reporters shouted out. 'Have you got anything to say, Inspector?'

'No comment!' called Hoot. He was in no mood for questions.

Efficient as ever, Jane steered Hoot away from the flock. Rounding the corner, she spotted a familiar figure fluttering shakily towards them.

'Sir, look it's Starling!'

'Florisa!' called Hoot. She looked much better now than when they'd last seen her at the East Oak. 'How's that wing? That sling looks uncomfortable.'

'I'm okay, sir. Just cuts and bruises, really. How did the case go? Did we get them?'

Hoot ruffled his wings and stared at his clawed feet. He didn't want to talk about the case. But Starling had a right to know.

'Well, Dwayne confessed to everything: stealing the painting, using the claw to leave a fake trail of goldfinch prints, hiding the painting in Da Finchi's workshop and kidnapping you. That stupid chaffinch is going to prison for a very long time.'

'And the Krows?' asked Florisa, holding her breath.

'Not guilty!' spat Hoot. 'There wasn't enough proof. And the poor jury were terrified when they saw Tommy and Terry in the dock. Not to mention their mother glaring at everyone from the gallery.'

Florisa felt sorry for Hoot – he looked old and tired. Starling had never seen him looking so miserable.

'Never mind, sir. At least we got Lord

Swan's precious painting back. And we arrested Dwayne. You should be proud of that, sir!'

From behind the two officers, came cackling laughter.

'Yes, Hoot, you should be really proud of yourself,' sniggered Tommy. 'Have a seed cake on us.'

While the officers had been talking, the Krows had been released from the court tree. They were grinning, enjoying every moment of their victory.

'No hard feelings, copper,' laughed Terry.

'There are a lot of hard feelings on my side Krow,' said Hoot, fixing the pair with a furious stare.

'Well there ain't nothing you can do. "Not guilty," the judge said!' laughed Tommy.

Tommy Krow swooped off, closely followed by his brother.

'Flapping felons!' shouted Hoot as the two black crows flew off. 'One day I'll get those Krow twins!'

Also from

MOGZILLA

Santa Claus is on a Diet!

By Nancy Scott-Cameron & illustrated
by Craig Conlan

Centuries of junk food and snacks have taken their toll on Santa's waistline. With narrow chimneys now a danger, Mrs Claus decides that it's time for Santa to change his diet and start exercising. The reindeer, keen to lighten their load, are only too happy to help. But there's a fatal flaw in their weight loss plan...

"A fun idea to get some important messages across." – Lorraine Kelly

ISBN: 9780954657697
AGE: 3 and up
PRICE: UK £9.99
FORMAT: 32 pages (hardback)
Full colour illustrations

It's 35 years since the iconic duo first brightened our teatimes. Now today's kids can follow the adventures of Roobarb, the optimistic green dog whose inventions often go spectacularly wrong - much to the delight of Custard, the sarcastic pink cat. The gentle wit and charm of these new Roobarb stories will feel instantly familiar.

'The gentle wit and charm of these new Roobarb stories will delight toddlers and parents... guaranteed to be laugh-out-loud funny.' - lovereading.co.uk

Price: £6.99
Extent: 34 pages of full-colour illustrations
For ages 4+

When there was a ballet
ISBN: 9781906132149

When Roobarb's trousers flew
ISBN: 9781906132149

When there was a pottery party
ISBN: 9781906132125

When Custard was grounded
ISBN: 9781906132101

When Roobarb found the hieroglyphics
ISBN: 9781906132118